Dimples Delight

D0711829

Dimples Delight

Frieda Wishinsky

with illustrations by
Louise-Andrée Laliberté

ORCA BOOK PUBLISHERS

National Library of Canada Cataloguing in Publication Data

Wishinsky, Frieda

Dimples delight / Frieda Wishinsky; with illustrations by Louise-Andrée Laliberté.

(Orca echoes)
ISBN 1-55143-362-1

1. Teasing--Juvenile fiction. I. Laliberté, Louise-Andrée II. Title. III. Series.

PS8595.I834D54 2005   jC813'.54   C2005-904059-9

First published in the United States: 2005

Library of Congress Control Number: 2005929686

Summary: Lawrence cannot bear Joe's teasing about his dimples, but nothing he does will make it stop.

Orca Book Publishers gratefully acknowledges the support for its publishing programs provided by the following agencies: the Government of Canada through the Department of Canadian Heritage's Book Publishing Industry Development Program (BPIDP), the Canada Council for the Arts, and the British Columbia Arts Council.

Design and layout: Lynn O'Rourke

Orca Book Publishers
Box 5626, Stn. B
Victoria, BC Canada
V8R 6S4

Orca Book Publishers
PO Box 468
Custer, WA USA
98240-0468

www.orcabook.com
Printed and bound in Canada
Printed on 50% post-consumer recycled paper,
processed chlorine free using vegetable, low VOC inks.

08 07 06 05 • 4 3 2 1

To Bill:
Without your love and dimples,
this story would never have come to be.

Chapter One
You're So Cute

On the first day of school, our new teacher, Ms. Parks, spotted me. I smiled at her. Right away, I knew that I had made a mistake.

"Will the boy in the blue sweater with the cute dimples in the second row please stand?" she boomed.

"Cute!" I groaned.

"Young man," Ms. Parks boomed again, "please stand."

Everyone's eyes were on me.

And then a rumbly voice from behind me said with a snicker, "Look at Dimple Boy!"

I knew that voice.

Everyone at school knew that voice.

It was Joe Morse.

"What's your name?" Ms. Parks asked me.

"Lawrence," I whispered.

"Speak up. Repeat your name loudly—with confidence," she said.

"Lawrence," I said.

"Thank you, Lawrence. You may sit down."

I sat down. My face burned.

I heard Joe laughing behind me. I turned around.

Joe was drilling holes into his cheeks with his fingers. He stuck out his tongue like he was going to be sick.

I wanted to say something, do something, anything, to make him stop. But what?

Ms. Parks handed out our new math book.

"Write your name in pencil on the inside cover," she told us.

I wrote my first name. On the first letter of my last name, my pencil point snapped like a twig.

I looked in my pencil case. My new baseball pencil and hot-dog eraser were gone. Eloise! My little sister Eloise always pokes into my stuff.

I looked around the classroom. The pencil sharpener was at the back of the room, past Joe's desk. The last thing I wanted to do was pass Joe.

"Psst, Stewart," I said.

My friend Stewart was sitting in the first row. He was drawing pictures of dinosaurs on the back of a notepad. Stewart loves dinosaurs.

Stewart didn't hear me, but Ms. Parks did.

"Is there something you'd like to share with the class, Lawrence?" she barked.

"No," I stammered.

"Then why aren't you busy writing?" she asked.

"My pencil broke," I said.

"Well, go to the back of the room and sharpen it," she said.

I stood up. My heart thumped. I walked fast.

Just as I thought I'd made it past Joe, I tripped. My head crashed into Lily Malone's like a rock.

"Ouch!" Lilly screamed.

"Ow!" I groaned.

Ms. Parks rushed to our side.

"Are you okay?" she asked.

"No," said Lilly. "He broke my head."

"Your head is not broken," said Ms. Parks. "But go to the office and get an ice pack so you don't have a bump. You too, Lawrence."

"I'm fine," I said, though my head ached.

"Are you sure, Lawrence?" asked Ms. Parks.

"Yes," I said.

I wasn't going to show Joe I was hurt. I wasn't going to give him anything else to tease me about.

"Is this what you tripped on?" Ms. Parks asked, picking up a book.

"Yes," I said.

Ms. Parks looked inside. "This belongs to you, Joe," she said. "How did it land on the floor?"

"I must have dropped it," said Joe. His voice was so sweet you could have eaten it on cereal.

Ms. Parks did not look impressed.

"Put it away," she said, handing Joe his book.

I walked to my seat. My head really hurt. But it hurt even more to know that Joe dropped the book on purpose. He enjoyed every minute of it.

Chapter Two
Forget About Him

At recess, Stewart and I played catch. I forgot about Joe for a few minutes.

Someone tapped me hard on my shoulder.

I spun around.

It was Joe.

"How's Dimples' little boo-boo?" he asked.

"Stop calling me that," I said.

"Now don't get so excited," he sneered. "It makes your face look like a tomato—a tomato with worm holes."

"Cut it out," I said, trying to stay cool. My face was burning again.

Joe laughed. "Come on, Dimple Boy. Don't cry." He blasted his words across the playground like a trumpet. Three boys stopped playing ball and laughed.

"Stop it!" I screamed.

"Relax, Dimple Boy," said Joe, "or your tomato face might explode. That would be gross!"

The three boys playing ball laughed louder. "Bye-bye, Dimple Boy," Joe called. He ran off to play with his friend Andrew.

I wanted to run, but I couldn't move my feet. I wanted to hide from the sound of those three boys laughing, but my feet wouldn't let me. All I could see was Joe's face.

Stewart yanked my sleeve. "Come on, Lawrence," he said. "Forget about him. He's a creep. Let's play ball."

"You're right," I said. "He is a creep."

I followed Stewart to a quiet spot at the back of the playground. We tossed a ball back and forth.

I tried to forget about Joe. By the end of recess, I almost had.

But at lunch, Joe was back. He leaned over my table. His stringy black hair almost dipped into my strawberry yogurt.

"Ugh!" he said, pointing to the yogurt. "Look at Dimples' girly food. It's all pink and gooey."

I ignored him, but the yogurt began to taste sour. I couldn't eat it. I put down my spoon.

"Hey," said Stewart. "Can I have your yogurt if you don't want it? I love yogurt. All my mom ever makes me are peanut-butter-and-jelly sandwiches on white bread."

"Sure," I said, handing Stewart the yogurt.

He wolfed it down in four spoonfuls. It's amazing how much Stewart can eat and still stay as skinny as a toothpick.

That's what he calls himself, The Amazing Food-Gobbling Toothpick.

"Don't let Joe bother you," Stewart mumbled between bites of his chocolate donut.

"But he does bother me. I hate it when he teases me," I said.

"He knows you hate it. You should see the happy look on his face. If you ignore him, he'll stop bugging you."

"How do I ignore him?" I asked Stewart.

"Watch me," said Stewart. "Call me a name."

"Hey, Toothpick."

Stewart didn't look at me. He just kept eating.

"Now call me a mean and nasty name. Something really bad," said Stewart.

"Hey, Slobber Mouth. Four Eyes. Pig Face," I said.

Stewart finished his donut and opened his milk carton as if he were deaf.

"That's good," he said. "Try a few more. Even meaner."

"Puke Head. Drool Face. Fat Lips," I said.

"Great," said Stewart. "Now I'll call you names so when Joe does, you'll be ready."

Stewart called me Bonzo Brain, Stupid Head, Dog Breath and twenty other disgusting names.

I ignored every one.

"See, it's not so hard," said Stewart.

"You're right," I said. "I can do it! I will do it! Starting tomorrow!"

17

Chapter Three
Wherever You Go

Today I will ignore Joe, I told myself all the way to school the next day.

Today, no matter what mean, gross names Joe calls me, I will be cold like an iceberg, deaf like a mummy, silent like a grave. Today I will do it!

I strode into class like a cowboy, ready to face the bad guys.

I looked around. No sign of Joe or Andrew.

I bent down to toss my schoolbag in my cubby. Something greasy touched my head. It was Joe. His hair dangled above me like black spaghetti.

He laughed.

"How wide are those dimples?" he said.

I ignored him.

"Come on, Andrew," said Joe. "Let's measure Lawrence's dimples."

Joe pulled a ruler out of his schoolbag.

"Voila!" he said, aiming his ruler at me like a sword.

I stood up and, cool as an iceberg, walked to my seat.

Joe was right behind me.

"Scared?" he said, waving his ruler in my face.

Deaf as a mummy, I said nothing.

"Dimple Boy is a chicken," sang Joe.

Silent as a grave, I did not answer.

Joe began clucking and circling me. He flapped his arms like a crazy chicken. Andrew clucked and flapped too.

I was still deaf and silent, but the cool was going. Fast. No matter how hard I tried not to let it, my face was burning.

The more they clucked and circled, the redder I got.

Lilly and Frank, who sat beside Joe, began to laugh. Sweat poured down my face like hot sauce. I didn't know how much more I could take.

Ms. Parks walked in. The clucking and flapping stopped.

For the next two hours I was safe.

Then it was recess.

As soon as the bell rang, Stewart dashed over to me.

"Follow me. Run!" Stewart whispered.

Stewart and I ran as fast as we could to the back of the schoolyard. We crawled under some bushes near a big shady maple.

We dropped to the ground.

"Stay here," said Stewart. "I'll see if we're safe."

Stewart crawled out to peek. He came back.

"No sign of them," he said.

"Phew," I said.

"Want to hear a dinosaur joke?" asked Stewart.

"Sure," I said.

"Why did the dinosaur paint his toenails ten different colors?"

"I don't know."

"To hide in the jelly-bean jar," said Stewart. He began to laugh.

I laughed too. I laughed harder and louder than I'd ever laughed at any dinosaur joke before. Soon Stewart and I were rolling on the ground, laughing.

"What's the matter with Dimples? Has he got ants in his pants?" said a voice.

Stewart and I stopped rolling and laughing.

Joe and Andrew crawled through the bushes.

"Hiding, Dimples?" asked Joe.

"From us?" asked Andrew.

We didn't answer.

"Don't try to hide, Dimples. Wherever you go, we'll find you," said Joe.

"We'll find you on top of the highest mountain. We'll find you at the bottom of the deepest ocean. We'll find you on the moon. We'll find you in... in..." said Andrew.

"We'll find you in your own room," said Joe, in a deep gangster voice.

Just then the school bell rang. Recess was over.

Stewart and I stood up.

We began to walk.

Joe and Andrew followed us.

We kept walking.

Joe and Andrew kept following.

We walked down the yard.

We walked up the stairs.

We walked into our classroom.

I sat in my seat and opened my math book.

Ms. Parks began the lesson. No matter how hard I tried to think about division, all I could think of was Joe and Andrew.

I had been cool. I had been deaf. I had been silent. I had ignored all the rotten, mean, disgusting things they had said.

But it hadn't done any good.

Chapter Four
Phone

That night the phone rang.

"Hi, cutie," said a high voice.

"Who is this?" I shouted.

"Want a kiss?" said the voice, cracking a little. A screechy kiss hissed through the phone.

I slammed it down.

Joe had said he would find me even in my room. And he had.

The phone rang again. I let it ring. Once. Twice. Three times.

"Please answer the phone," my mother called from the basement.

"I'm sure it's a wrong number," I called back. The phone rang again.

"It might be important. I can't go to the phone now," said my mother. "Eloise stuck a wad of toilet paper down the toilet. It's running over."

The phone rang again. And again. And again. Joe wasn't going to stop.

"Lawrence!" called my mother.

I had no choice. I picked up the phone.

"Hello," I said.

No one answered. I could hear someone breathing.

"Who's there?" I asked.

The breathing got louder. Creepier.

"What do you want?" I shouted.

"You," said the voice, laughing so loudly that I had to hold the phone away from my ear.

I hung up.

Joe was trying to drive me crazy. Well, he wouldn't. I wouldn't let him. The next time he called, I'd tell him off but good.

"Who was it?" called my mom.

"Wrong number," I said.

The phone rang again.

Okay. Here goes. I took a long, deep breath. I picked up the phone. "Hello," I said calmly.

Someone coughed into the phone.

"I know it's you, you big creep," I said and slammed the phone down.

The phone rang again.

I picked it up.

"Lawrence, what's the matter with you?" said the voice.

The voice did not belong to Joe.

It belonged to my Aunt Molly.

"Did you just call?" I asked.

"Yes, I did, and you called me a creep. How could you? How could you?"

"But Aunt Molly," I said.

It was too late. She hung up. She called later and told my mother. Mom was angry with me.

"But Mom, please listen," I said.

At last she did.

"Oh," she said. "I see. Well, ignore Joe."

"I have," I said. "But it's not helping."

"Give it a little more time. Believe me. He'll grow tired of bugging you."

Yeah, sure. Maybe when I'm ninety, I thought, but not now. Now he's having too much fun.

Chapter Five
The Rash

When I woke up the next morning, the first thing I thought of was Joe. I didn't want to think about him. But there he was. His face hung over me like a black cloud. His screechy voice rang in my ear like a fire bell.

I blinked and shook my head to get his voice and face out of my mind.

It helped a little, but what helped more was the clock.

Nuts! It was 8:30! I had fifteen minutes to get out of the house and dash to school.

"Breakfast, Lawrence," my mother called.

"In a minute," I answered.

I leaped into my jeans and pulled a T-shirt over my head.

I ran to the bathroom and brushed my teeth and combed my hair. Then I glanced in the mirror.

"Yikes!" I shrieked.

"What's the matter?" called my mom. She dashed into the bathroom.

I couldn't talk. I could just point to my face.

There, where my dimples usually are, were two large dots, two fire-engine-red dots.

"Eloise!" I gasped. "How could she? How did she?"

"Eloise," said my mother, "come here, please."

Eloise hopped into the bathroom in her bunny pajamas.

She looked at me and giggled.

"Eloise," said my mother, "you are never to draw on anyone's face."

"But Lawrence looks cute like that," said Eloise. "And I didn't wake him up. He was asleep the whole time."

31

"Lawrence does not think he looks cute like that," said Mom." Faces are not for drawing. Use paper next time "

"I didn't have any paper," Eloise said. She giggled again.

"Ask for paper," said Mom.

"I couldn't," said Eloise. "You were sleeping."

"Mom!" I said. "I'm late. I have to get this stuff off my face."

Mom handed me a wet washcloth with soap on it.

"It should fade in time. Rub," she said.

I rubbed. I rubbed up. I rubbed down. I rubbed across. But the more I rubbed, the worse my face looked. The red dots smeared into a mess. I looked like an alien. I looked worse than an alien.

"Hurry up, Lawrence," called Mom. "It's almost nine."

I had no choice. I had to leave. I grabbed my bag and ran.

The bell rang as I slid into my seat.

Chapter Six
It's Nothing

"Our first lesson this morning will be science," said Ms. Parks. She held up a huge picture of a plant. "This is the stem and these are the petals and… Lawrence, what happened to your face?"

"Nothing, Ms. Parks," I said.

"You look terrible, Lawrence. I think you should see the nurse."

"I feel fine. It's nothing," I said.

"Lawrence, go to the nurse," Ms. Parks said right back.

As I walked out of the class, I could hear Joe and Andrew laughing.

The nurse's office was down the hall. I walked slowly. I looked at every picture on the wall between my class and her office.

I knocked.

"Come in," she said.

The nurse was sitting at a desk, writing on cards.

She looked up. "What seems to be the problem?" she asked.

"I have a little rash. It's nothing," I said.

"Let me take a look," she said.

She stood up and walked over to me. She peered at my face.

"What did you have for breakfast?"

"A glass of milk," I said.

"Chocolate milk?"

"No. Plain."

"What about last night? Potato chips, pretzels, French fries—peanuts?"

"Nothing special or different," I said.

"Hmm," she said. She turned my face from left to right. Then she rubbed my face lightly with a cotton ball dipped in alcohol. The cotton turned pink.

"You have marker on your face!" she said. "Why didn't you tell me?"

"I...I..."

"You kids. I'll never understand you. Why did you write on your face, and with marker, of all things?"

"I didn't," I said. "My sister did." I told her about Eloise.

"I see," she said. She smiled for the first time. "I'll write your teacher a note."

"Please don't tell her. Can't you just tell her I'm allergic to something? I could be allergic to sardines. Sardines make me turn colors."

"I can't write that if it's not true," she said. "Don't worry, though. I won't give you away. I have a little sister too. Here's some cream to help take off the marker."

I thanked her and rubbed in a bit of the cream. It took off some of the marker, but not all.

"Give it time. The marker will fade. By tomorrow or the next day, you'll hardly see it."

I walked slowly back to class. Tomorrow! The next day! I thought. My face is going to look like this all day!

I handed Ms. Parks the note from the nurse. "Thank you," she said. "You may sit down."

I slipped into my seat. I saw Joe poke Andrew in the arm. They both stared at me. They stared at me for the rest of the lesson. I stared at my science book. I learned all the parts of a flower. Ms. Parks talked on.

The recess bell rang.

Everyone raced to the door. Stewart and I were halfway down the hall when Joe caught up with us.

"Look, everybody! Dimples has a disease!" Joe shouted.

Twenty kids turned and stared.

Joe brushed against my shirt.

"Help!" he screeched, jumping away. "I touched him. It's the plague! I'll catch it. I'm going to die!"

"Come on. Ignore him," said Stewart. "Let's play catch."

I played catch, but I kept dropping the ball as if it was on fire. I felt like the whole playground was laughing at me and my face.

Chapter Seven
Smile Control

I was glad to get home that day. I was glad that the ink was fading. Maybe by tomorrow it would be all gone.

But Joe would still be there. My dimples would still be there. They would never go away.

I closed my eyes. I wished that my dimples would disappear. I wished that I would wake up with smooth cheeks.

I wished I had someone else's face.

I knew that wishing wouldn't help.

Then I had an idea. My dimples only showed when I smiled. If I stopped smiling, no one would see them. Maybe they would forget I had dimples. Maybe they would leave me alone.

I decided to practice that night. My whole family, including Aunt Molly, was going to watch a funny movie.

"Five minutes till movie time!" sang my dad.

My mother turned down the lights. "Aunt Molly," I whispered, "I'm sorry about the phone the other night."

"I forgive you," said Aunt Molly. She pinched my cheek with her long red nails. "But just this once."

I winced. "Smile Control" was about to begin.

So was the movie.

Five minutes later, two men in the movie fell into a puddle of mud. Everyone laughed—everyone but me. I held the laugh back. I sucked in my cheeks. I puckered my lips. A low cough-like sound came out.

I looked around to see if anyone had heard me, but everyone was too busy watching to notice.

The second time something funny happened, it caught me by surprise. I pulled back the laugh that tried to escape. The strangest sound, something between a snort and a hiccup, popped out.

This time my whole family turned around.

"Are you sick?" asked my mother.

"Caught a cold?" asked my father.

"Cover your mouth when you cough, dear," said Aunt Molly.

"Stop making dumb noises," said Eloise.

"I'm fine," I said.

My family turned back to the movie. For the rest of the show, I didn't laugh. It was hard, and it wasn't fun.

But I did it. I made "Smile Control" work. And tomorrow at school I'd make it work again.

Chapter Eight
I Can Do It

A block from school I saw Stewart walking toward me.

"Look what I can do!" he said. He twisted his tongue till it almost touched his ear. " I practiced all night. Pretty funny, right?"

"Right," I said.

"So why aren't you laughing?" he asked.

"I am laughing, inside," I said.

"That's crazy. Listen to this. Why did the dinosaur order spaghetti at the restaurant?" asked Stewart.

"I don't know."

"He didn't. Dinosaurs never eat in restaurants," said Stewart. He howled.

I didn't howl. I didn't laugh. I didn't even smile.

"Why aren't you laughing?" Stewart asked. "Didn't you like the joke?"

"I liked it," I said.

"Then why didn't you laugh?"

"I was laughing inside again," I said.

"Sure. Sure," said Stewart. "If your best friend won't laugh when you work all night to stretch your tongue to your ear or tell funny jokes, who will?"

Stewart looked so hurt that I had to tell him about "Smile Control."

He listened. Then he laughed.

"What's so funny?" I asked.

"That's the craziest idea I ever heard. How can anyone stay serious all day?"

"I can. Just watch me."

And I did.

I didn't laugh when Patty told Ms. Parks the parakeet pooped on her homework.

I didn't laugh when I saw Greg's socks, one green and the other white.

I didn't even laugh when Howie got so mad at Billy that he dumped orange juice down Billy's shirt.

"I told you I could do it," I said to Stewart at lunch.

Just then, Joe leaned over our table.

"What's the matter, Dimple Boy? You look sad. Are you gonna cry?"

I didn't answer.

"Well I hope not," said Joe. "I'd hate to see those big holes get all wet and soggy. It would make me sick." And then Joe did his throw-up face again.

I wanted to hit him, but I couldn't.

"Smile Control" was a waste.

Joe was never going to forget about my dimples. Never.

Chapter Nine
Oh, That Stewart!

It was only the second week, but I felt like I'd been in school for a year.

I hated it. I wanted to hide or run away.

It was like this movie I once saw about jail.

In the movie, this one guy is innocent, but he's still accused of a crime and thrown in jail. In jail, these two mean guys hound him. The guards won't help. One day, the guy can't take it any more. He leaps from the jail wall into a moat and swims to safety.

The guy in the movie escaped to freedom.

I couldn't leap into a moat and escape to freedom. I couldn't get away from Joe and Andrew.

All that recess, Stewart and I played catch. I kept dropping the ball. I kept seeing Joe's face. I kept expecting Joe to show up and tease me. I kept expecting him to call me names and make the kids laugh at me.

"What's the matter, Lawrence?" asked Stewart.

"I don't feel that well today," I said.

I think Stewart knew what I meant. He didn't ask anything else.

I was glad that, after recess, Joe had to go to the dentist. His dad picked him up at the classroom.

"What's taking you so long?" his dad barked as Joe picked up his papers and books. "You're always so slow and clumsy. I don't have all day."

Joe tried to hide his face as his dad spoke. I could see his face turning red. Joe stuffed the rest of his papers into his bag. He hurried out of the room with his dad still frowning behind him.

For the next few hours I relaxed. But I knew Joe wasn't going to go to the dentist every day.

The home bell rang.

Outside, Patty tapped Stewart on the back.

"Heard any good dinosaur jokes lately, Toothpick?" she asked.

Stewart smiled.

"Yeah!" he said. "Why did the dinosaur sleep in the haystack?"

"I don't know," aid Patty.

"Because his new bed hadn't come yet."

Patty and I laughed.

"That was pretty good, Toothpick," she said.

Stewart smiled. It was weird. Patty called Stewart "Toothpick," but Stewart didn't mind. He liked being called Toothpick.

I thought about it all the way home. A block from home, I knew. The answer was so clear. I couldn't believe I hadn't thought of it before.

No one teases Stewart because Stewart teases himself!

Stewart calls himself a toothpick.

When Stewart got his new glasses, he was the first to laugh at how thick they were. "You've got to see these telescopes," he said.

The whole class laughed with Stewart. The next day, three kids in class said they wanted glasses as "cool" as Stewart's glasses.

It was no fun teasing Stewart.

But it was fun teasing me!

I had to take the fun out.

I had to get used to my dimples. Maybe even like them.

I looked in the hall mirror.

I smiled as wide as I could.

My dimples were two holes. But what's so bad about holes?

Holes are nice. Holes are different. Holes are fun!

It all depends on how you see them.

Chapter Ten
Eloise

"What are you doing, Lawrence?" asked Eloise.

I didn't know what to say. I couldn't tell Eloise my plan. I stopped smiling into the mirror.

"Why don't you smile anymore?" asked Eloise. "You're always so grumpy now."

"I'm not grumpy," I told her. " See." I smiled a big smile right at her.

"Hey, Lawrence," she said. "I think your dimples are bigger. They look like caves. You could put peanuts in there. Can I see if a peanut fits?"

"No," I said.

"How about a raisin? I bet a raisin would fit."

"No," I said. I went to the kitchen to get a snack. Eloise followed me.

"How about a chocolate chip? You could eat it when you got hungry."

"Go away, Eloise," I shouted.

"You said you weren't going to be grumpy any more. You lied. You're still grumpy."

Eloise stormed out of the kitchen.

The doorbell rang. It was Aunt Molly. Now I'd really get to test my dimple plan.

"Hi, Aunt Molly," I said, giving her a big smile.

"Well hello, darling," she said. She pinched my cheek. "You're much more cheerful today."

Her pinch stung like a needle. I kept smiling.

"Yes, I'm in a much better mood today," I told her.

"Well, Lawrence," she cooed, pinching my cheeks again, "I love your dimples. I always say to your mother, 'No one has dimples like Lawrence.'"

"I know," I said.

I winced again. My cheeks burned from Aunt Molly's nails. Why did she have to have such long, sharp nails? Maybe my face was bleeding.

My face was aching from all the smiling and pinching, so I stopped smiling. I thought I should save all my smiles for Joe anyway.

They had to be special smiles for Joe. I had to smile as if I loved my dimples. I had to smile as if I wished everyone in the world had dimples. I had to smile as if, no matter what Joe said about me or my dimples, I didn't care.

Would it work? Maybe Joe would find something else to tease me about. Maybe he'd tease me about being short. Maybe he'd tease me about how my hair got curly when it rained. Maybe he'd tease me about the small space between my two front teeth.

Maybe nothing I'd do would work.

Tomorrow I would know.

Chapter Eleven
Dumb Holes

The next morning, Joe poked me in the stomach.

"We're measuring your holes today," he said in his gangster voice, waving his ruler.

"Wait!" I said.

I reached into my cubby and pulled out my ruler. I pulled out a washable red pen and made a dot in each of my dimples.

"Voila!" I said. I smiled my widest smile.

I placed my ruler on my face. I felt where my dimple began and where it ended.

"Perfect! A matching pair," I said.

Joe stared at me. His tongue hung in his mouth as if he had lost the power to speak.

The bell rang.

We sat down.

My heart pounded.

I'd won round one. Round two was coming.

It came at recess.

"Let's play catch," said Stewart.

Stewart and I threw the ball back and forth. I felt a hard jab in my ribs. It was Joe.

"People with dumb holes are dumb people," he said.

"Dimples are not dumb holes. They're wonderful holes," I told him. "They're perfect for...for... storing peanuts."

"What are you talking about?" Joe said.

"Or storing raisins and chocolate chips. I can store them in my dimples and have them later for snack. Want me to store some for you?"

"That is gross," said Joe. "I wouldn't touch a chocolate chip you'd stored in your sweaty cheek."

"The sweat gives them extra flavor," I said.

"Everyone knows the best-tasting peanuts and chips have a little sweat on them," said Stewart.

"You two are crazy," Joe said.

"You don't have to believe me or Stewart," I said, smiling again. "But it's a known fact."

Stewart threw me a ball, and I caught it.

"Didn't you hear me?" Joe's voice rose higher and higher. "You're dumb. Stupid. Crazy. An idiot with two holes."

"Sure, I heard you," I said. I laughed. "You're loud."

"You're nuts," said Joe. "You should get your head examined."

"I've had my head examined. It's in great shape," I said.

"Let's get away from these two crazy dumb-heads," Joe said to Andrew.

And then, like a bad smell, they were gone.

Billy and Howie ran over.

"That was great, Lawrence," they said. "You really got Joe."

I smiled. "Want to play catch?" I asked them.

"Sure."

We played. And it was amazing. The balls sank into my hand as if a magnet pulled them there. I could catch anything: fly balls, grounders, curve balls, balls shot from a rocket!

With each catch, my smile grew wider.

"You're good, Dimple Boy," said Stewart, patting me on the back.

"You too, Toothpick!"

Orca Echoes

The Paper Wagon
martha attema
Graham Ross, illustrator

The Big Tree Gang
Jo Ellen Bogart
Dean Griffiths, illustrator

Ghost Wolf
Karleen Bradford
Allan Cormack and Deborah
Drew-Brook, illustrators

*Jeremy and the
Enchanted Theater*
Becky Citra
Jessica Milne, illustrator

Sam and Nate
PJ Sarah Collins
Katherine Jin, illustrator

*Down the Chimney with
Googol and Googolplex*
Nelly Kazenbroot

*Under the Sea with
Googol and Googolplex*
Nelly Kazenbroot

The Birthday Girl
Jean Little
June Lawrason, illustrator

The True Story of George
Ingrid Lee
Stéphane Denis, illustrator

George Most Wanted
Ingrid Lee
Stéphane Denis, illustrator

A Noodle Up Your Nose
Frieda Wishinsky
Louise-Andrée Laliberté,
illustrator

A Bee in Your Ear
Frieda Wishinsky
Louise-Andrée Laliberté, illustrato